I'm There For You

C.S. Meyering

authorHOUSE®

AuthorHouse™
1663 Liberty Drive
Bloomington, IN 47403
www.authorhouse.com
Phone: 1 (800) 839-8640

Published by AuthorHouse 07/28/2018

ISBN: 978-1-5462-4630-5 (sc)
ISBN: 978-1-5462-4629-9 (e)

Print information available on the last page.

Any people depicted in stock imagery provided by Getty Images are models, and such images are being used for illustrative purposes only. Certain stock imagery © Getty Images.

This book is printed on acid-free paper.

Because of the dynamic nature of the Internet, any web addresses or links contained in this book may have changed since publication and may no longer be valid. The views expressed in this work are solely those of the author and do not necessarily reflect the views of the publisher, and the publisher hereby disclaims any responsibility for them.

For kids,
may you always have someone there for you.

Jack

An Ordinary Thursday

I wonder what people mean when they say, "It's just another normal day." Is their normal, like my normal? Or is their day normal and mine, well, mine is something other than normal? Take yesterday, for instance. I got up late because my alarm clock doesn't work, and hasn't for weeks now. I told Mom about it, but she didn't even look at me when I explained why I needed a new clock. I don't know if she heard me or not.

Am I supposed to know when to wake up, like I have a special power or something? I do try though, because I like going to school. People care about me there or at least they pretend to, and that's enough for me. I like being with lots of people. It's so different than being home where I don't see or talk with anyone for days. The T.V. used to be my buddy, but now that's broken too. I guess that's a good way to describe my life - broken. I feel that way most days, definitely not like I am whole, complete, or normal.

Yesterday morning I woke to find the sun was already up. I flew out of bed and ran into the kitchen, stepping on Alice's tail. She let out a hiss and sank her teeth into my tender, bare foot. Yowza! That helped me move faster! I glanced up at the kitchen wall where the clock hung above the sink. A clock that looked like a twisted chicken: a sad, scrawny, long necked chicken, with a circle of numbers on it's wing. The hands resembled creepy chicken feet. It was grotesquely familiar, and I wondered how someone would decide to make something so bizarre. Why would someone BUY it, I wondered even more. With those creepy chicken "feet hands" at 7 and 4, I realized I had to be at school in 10 minutes or it would be another tardy. I didn't need another one of those. I already had earned more than allowed for the whole school year.

I flew back to my room and slipped into jeans that were sprawled out on the floor like legs in a crime scene photo I'd seen on T.V. I dug through the pile of clothes on my closet floor and found an old Batman sweatshirt and some smelly socks that didn't match. Those would have to do. I grabbed my shoes by the door and took off. I sprinted down the driveway and across the street. I cut between houses hoping maybe, just maybe, I could make it to school before the bell....

As I flung open the front door of Pine Hills Elementary and Middle School, the bell began screeching like a huge crow swooping down to peck my eyes out.

"Well, good morning Mr. Wilson!" I heard as I flew by the office.

The voice came from Mr. Lily, our assistant principal. Yes, Mr. LILY. Being named after a flower did not match this man with an average face, worn and wrinkled. Even with his authoritative presence, there was something special about Mr. Lily. Not that I could find words to describe him, but there was something about his eyes.

"I was....trying to.....get to class on time, really....I was, Mr. Lily." I sputtered as my heavy breathing made it difficult to get the words out.

"I'll walk with you." he calmly stated, as Mr. Lily caught up with me.

I slowed my pace to a stride matching his. "I'm sorry Mr. Lily, really I am. I tried not to be tardy today." He looked at me with those eyes. He saw ME, I could feel it. We walked the rest of the way to my classroom in silence. A silence that returned my heartbeat and breathing back to a normal rate.

Kids had found their rooms, and only the squeak of my shoes, wet from the dew on the grass, filled the hallway.

By the time we reached my classroom, it didn't matter that my morning had been crazy. As I entered the room, I saw Mr. Lily nod to Ms. Franklin. She continued her morning instructions uninterrupted as she responded with a nod and small grin. Trying to make myself small, I slunk over to my desk, sinking down in the seat. I didn't want anyone to know I'd been escorted to the room once again.

My desk felt familiar and comforted me. The desk was big, allowing me to slide around easily. It was a great spot too, being just five steps from the door, with three desks in front of me and one behind. I could see Ms. Franklin if I tilted my head to the left, but if I sat up straight or moved my body slightly to the right, I was hidden and hopefully unnoticed. I had a good view of the clock so I could count down the minutes to lunch when I was back here for English class fourth period. Just sitting in this desk made me feel better.

I glanced up at the schedule Ms. Franklin had written on the board. I could count on that. I wondered if I was supposed to have done math homework last night. Yesterday seemed so long ago. As I tried to remember, I heard Ms. Franklin's soft voice as she talked about making this a good day. Maybe life was better for her. Maybe she went to a real home each night. One with hugs, always enough food, people talking and listening. Things all happening in a logical order - kind of like in our classroom. Everything we do here seems so organized - planned and meant to happen. How does she make that work? Is that normal?

As I allowed myself to wander off in thought, the bell rang. It startled me so much that I lurched forward in my desk and clunked my knee on a piece of metal that dug into my pant leg, creating a hole in my jeans. I tried not to let anyone see how much it hurt as I scrambled to get up and out the door to my first period class in room 217 - math. I sure hoped I could figure things out better today. Learning to multiply fractions was driving me crazy!

The day seemed to last as long as two, but finally the last bell of the day rang. I took a breath, sat and stared ahead for a few extra seconds, then got out of my desk. Kids rushed around me and into the hall like kittens scurrying to a fresh bowl of milk.

What should I do next? Head home, or hang around school a bit? The school was so quiet after kids left. It was awesome. I decided to walk along the empty halls, my footsteps making tiny echoes. The solid cement walls made me feel safe and protected. I looked for familiar details along the walls as I meandered down each hallway: a crack about knee high following the fifth column of cement blocks past the science room, a huge dead spider smashed on the window of the music room, (that had been there the past 13 days), and a poster for the fall play that had happened exactly three weeks and two days ago, the top right corner flapping over part of Cinderella's face. I loved this time. I didn't have to think a single important thought. Meaningless details were enough to fill my mind and make me feel content.

Feeling lighter, I started on my way home, taking the long way. The sidewalks had gathered crunch-filled leaves throughout the day, and I loved the sound as I stomped and shuffled my way down the block. The breeze on my face was soft and smelled of autumn.

An Unexpected Visitor

Once I got home, I decided to get homework out of the way. As I worked on my math, things seemed to be clicking a little more than usual. I was glad. Sometimes I let this math stuff drive me nuts. If only I would just be patient and keep trying instead of getting frustrated right away. Then it's like my brain shuts down and I can't think clearly.

Feeling upbeat, I decided to check out the fridge to see what my supper might be. Hmmmm.....a piece of moldy cheese, some rubbery celery, and a piece of bologna that looked a little too shiny. No thanks. I opened the cupboard door to my left, and ta da, three cans stared at me! I grabbed a can of pork and beans. A good source of protein I told myself. I pulled the can opener out of the sink and opened the can containing my gourmet meal. I grabbed a spoon lying on the cabinet and took the can up to my bed where I managed to scarf down the whole thing in seconds.

Sitting on the bed wondering what to do next, I glanced out the window and saw Mr. Lily walking down the sidewalk across the street. As I watched him, he crossed the street and continued walking STRAIGHT TOWARD MY HOUSE! Whoa! What if he was coming here? Why would he do that? I closed my eyes and waited.

Then there it was, a gentle rap, rap, rap on the front door. I thought for a moment if I held real still, Mr. Lily would go away and I could just wonder what he had wanted. No, I couldn't do that. I was just too curious. I moved to the front door, trying to tidy up a bit as I went. As I opened the door, I could see Mr. Lily turning to leave the porch.

"Hey Mr. Lily!" I shouted, maybe with a little too much enthusiasm.

"Well, hello Mr. Wilson!" I heard while I looked into those familiar smiling eyes. "I happened to be in the neighborhood." he lied. "I thought I'd stop and see if you were planning to be on time for school tomorrow."

"I want to be on time everyday Mr. Lily, really I do. I just don't always get up on time. You see my alarm clock hasn't been working, and......"

Mr. Lily began to chuckle as I tried to justify my consistent tardiness.

I noticed he was trying to peer through the screen door into the house, so I decided to open the door and go outside to talk to him on the front porch. He seemed okay with that because he sat down on the top step and patted the space next to him as a signal for me to join him. MY PRINCIPAL IS SITTING ON MY PORCH STEPS! Who is going to see us and use this moment to tease me tomorrow at school? I paused for a moment, unsure of myself and what I should do. I decided to take a seat and see what this unexpected visit was all about. Mr. Lily looked at me, and I knew I had made the right choice to sit down and listen.

"Jack, I am in need of some help and I thought you might be the person who could help me."

Mr. Lily needed MY help? This all seemed too weird to me.

"I am worried about one of my first graders." Mr. Lily blurted out. "He is so scared at school, and he is unable to stop crying long enough to show us the great work he can do."

I realized I had been holding my breath, and let out a large sigh.

"I have tried many things to make Zachary, that's the first grader's name, feel comfortable and nothing seems to be helping him. This morning when we walked to class, you got me thinking. You are one of those students that could help Zachary feel comfortable at school and help him work up to his full potential. You see, Zachary has had some scary stuff happen in his life. It makes him afraid to try anything new. Do you think you'd be willing to be, like a big buddy to him Jack? Help him to realize that school isn't such a bad place to be?"

I spent what seemed like a long time letting this information run through my head......young boy.....scary stuff......afraid to try......all too familiar to me. Could I possibly help another person with things I struggled with? Memories filled my brain and I could feel my muscles tightening as my body began to curl forward. I grabbed my knees and pulled them to my chest.

Mr. Lily brought me back to the moment as he asked, "Jack, what do you think?"

"Mr. Lily, I, I, I don't think I'd be very good at, at you know, helping Zachary."

Mr. Lily sat and looked at me for a few seconds and then confidently stated, "Jack, I know you are probably the BEST person in the whole school to help Zachary. Would you please think about it?"

My brain was fuzzy, and my thoughts mixed up. I didn't know if I could respond. I turned my head slightly toward Mr. Lily, nodded, then looked back down at my knees.

Mr. Lily gently patted my back twice while softly whispering, "I know you can do it Jack. Zachary needs you."

He NEEDS me? I could never be counted on for anything. As thoughts flooded my head, I had to close my eyes to keep them inside. I lost all track of time. I don't know if I sat there for a minute or an hour, but when I opened my eyes I was sitting by myself on the top step of the porch. The breeze was chilly, and I could hear the sharp rustle of leaves blowing down the sidewalk.

A Different Kind of Morning

I woke with a start, sitting straight up in bed. I wondered what time it was. I ran quickly to check the twisted chicken, and saw that it was 6:00! Had I ever gotten up this early? I crawled back into bed, but all I could think of was making sure that today I got to school on time. I got out of bed and took a shower. I brushed my teeth, combed my hair, and made sure I found socks that matched. I chose a pair of jeans that didn't have any stains, and found a clean red T-shirt hiding in the back of my top drawer.

Checking the mirror, I gave myself a little smile. "Not bad." I murmured aloud.

As I strutted into the kitchen, I felt different somehow. I didn't know why, but I kind of liked this new feeling. I searched through a few cupboards and all I found were more cans of baked beans. No beans for breakfast, I decided. There was some change in a cup on the counter, and I scavenged 98 cents. Maybe that would be enough to buy a breakfast sandwich at the corner gas station. I was feeling hungry, but if I left now I was sure to be at school before anyone else. I decided to shove the coins into my pants pocket and wait a little while before I headed out.

I looked around the kitchen. There were dirty cans with bits of food left inside, sitting on the table and in the sink. On the floor, leaves were scattered that must have come in on my shoes or blew in when the door was open. As I glanced in the corner of the room, I noticed a little black fuzzy shape. When I got closer to investigate, I could see that it was a mouse, dead, with it's hair matted down where Alice must have carried it in her mouth. She probably brought it inside to keep as a snack for later. Oh, Alice......

Where was Alice? I hadn't seen her this morning and she hadn't slept with me last night. At least I don't remember her jumping on the bed. Out prowling around the town, I figured.

I decided to clean up a little with my extra time this morning. I threw away pieces of can labels and other paper scraps scattered over the table. I washed out the cans and took them outside to the recycling bin. The dishrag smelled worse than dead mouse so I used it to pick up the mouse, keeping my hands from touching the sticky rodent. I threw that tidy little package into the garbage can under the sink. I took the whole garbage can outside to the dumpster and felt a little sad getting rid of a meal Alice probably had worked hard to secure. I found a new dishrag in the third drawer underneath a box of tin foil, and got it wet. I wiped off the round table and all the countertops, rinsing it out when it got all gummy. Some spots had to be scrubbed more than once, but by the time I was done and looked over my work, I must say it looked lots better. I found a broom in the hall closet and swept up the leaves and other questionable pieces of things scattered over the floor. Some spots were sticky, and I used the dishcloth to scrub away whatever was making my feet stick to the floor. Once that was finished, I stood back to admire my work. Wow! Maybe I could go into the housecleaning business and make some big bucks. That thought made me shake my head. No, thank you!

My stomach started to growl, and I decided it was time to find something to eat. I quickly opened the window above the sink about six inches to let Alice squeeze through whenever she decided to come home. Hopefully without any more dead animal treats! I ran to my bedroom, grabbed my backpack and started toward the front door.

Checking the chicken, I realized I still had lots of time before school started, so I didn't need to hurry. That was a different feeling, not hurrying. Hurrying was "my usual" each morning on school days. Running through yards, trying to find new shortcuts, hoping to get to school before the bell so Mr. Lily wouldn't have to escort me through the halls. Mr. Lily....I had almost forgotten about him coming to my house yesterday. Had he? Was it a dream, or did I really sit on the front porch steps with him, listening to him ask for MY help?

I went out the front door, and onto the porch. Yup, this is where we sat talking yesterday, I was almost sure of it. I couldn't remember if I had agreed to helping that boy he was talking about...Timothy,.....Bradley,.... Zachary? In fact, I don't remember Mr. Lily leaving.

I walked slowly to use up the time remaining before school. As I entered the gas station on the corner, I saw a sign, *Breakfast Sandwiches - Half Price.* Fifty cents for a sandwich was a bonus, so I eyed them all and chose one that had ham and cheese. That would give me, hmmm......48 cents left. The smallest bottle of orange juice was 50 cents, so I grabbed that as well and went up to the counter. I remembered there was always a little dish of pennies next to the check out person, and I quickly grabbed two to move my 48 cents up to 50 to cover the juice.

I handed the coins to the lady behind the counter, who glanced at my purchases and said, "Exact change! That's just what I like!" and gave me a big smile! Today was sure going great! If I was old enough, I'd buy a lottery ticket!

I savored my breakfast as I strolled with an air of confidence the rest of the way to school. I shoved the wrapper in my coat pocket and used my sleeve to clean off any sandwich left on my face. Taking long strides down the sidewalks, crisp morning air filled my lungs.

Walking through the front doors of the school building I got a strange feeling. I couldn't remember ever "walking" through those doors. My usual entrance was racing up the sidewalk to the school, flinging the door open as I flew through, wondering if the morning bell had rung yet. This was such an unfamiliar feeling as I took in the different approach to my day. The halls were full of kids, laughing and grouped together like flocks of birds throughout the hallways. Some moved slowly towards their homerooms, some huddled in groups of two or three sitting cross legged against the walls, trying to frantically complete forgotten or ignored homework. Some shared answers while others scribbled them down, gobbling them up as if they were starving for the information being provided. I wandered through the groups somehow feeling connected, although I spoke to no one, and no one spoke to me.

As I walked into Ms. Franklin's room, the bell rang. I sat down in my usual spot to watch the other kids frantically rush in. I listened to loud voices change to whispers, as if the classroom doorway was a magic portal that automatically minimized sound. That thought made me smile.

Shawn walked past, smiled back at me and said, "Hey!" I gave him a nod. Shawn and I had spent many days together after school the beginning of last year. We did homework, walked his golden retriever Max, and played in the park. Then he moved to a foster home in a different town and our friendship had disappeared. This year he was back. We only had homeroom together, and with me always flying in at the last minute, we hadn't had time to talk to each other. To be honest, I had forgotten about us doing so much together last year.

While deep in the thoughts of walking that huge dog of his, and how he would pull us down the road chasing squirrels, Mr. Lily startled me by putting his hand on my shoulder. "Looks like you were having a great daydream Jack." he chuckled. I could feel my face get red. "Glad to see you here on time today, young man." He spoke quietly into my ear. "Just wondering if you could meet Zachary and I at lunch time today."

So, it hadn't been a dream. "Sure, Mr. Lily." I barely whispered. I didn't want anyone to know I was going to be hanging out with a first grader - like they cared. Still, I didn't feel like getting teased about not having friends my own age, so I had to find a first grader to spend time with. I wondered if Mr. Lily had thought about that. I made a mental note - I would need to make sure our meetings were in places I wouldn't be seen.

I started to feel nervous about being responsible for turning this kid around. Mr. Lily must think I can do it, but what did he really know about me anyway. I didn't hear anything that Ms. Franklin said during homeroom, as my thoughts were about how I could possibly help Zachary when I was so unsure of myself.

My morning classes seemed to drag on, and it was hard to keep my thoughts on what the teachers were saying. Everything was like a slow motion video, the kind where the voices were all garbled and drawn out like whales trying to communicate with each other. I felt nervous thinking that I, Jack Wilson, chronic latecomer with a life, "not so normal," could do anything to be a good influence on a scared first grade boy. What did I know about being a role model? Maybe I would tell Mr. Lily I just couldn't do it. Maybe I would go to the nurse and say I was sick and needed to go home. I am not someone you can count on, don't people know that?

While I kept trying to think of excuses, the time ticked away and my stomach felt queasy. I knew it was a nervous thing, but now I could be telling the truth if I told the nurse I didn't feel well. I put my head on the desk and began to breathe slowly in and out to help myself calm down. Breathe in, one...two...three, and breathe out, one...two...three. The counselor had told me about using the breathing stuff when I used to get angry or worried. It had helped and I guess it was worth trying now.

I had really liked seeing Miss Lor every week. She listened and helped me learn how to handle stuff. This year when school started, I went and asked the secretary in the office if I could talk to Miss Lor. I had things I needed to tell her. I was told that she didn't work in our building anymore. I wondered if there was a new counselor, but I really didn't want to see anyone new. I felt disappointed, but just chalked it up to the way things go for me. Anyone that I need never stays around for very long.

Now what was I thinking about before.....oh yeah, counting to help myself calm down and stop feeling upset. That was something I could share with Zachary if he was feeling scared at school. Oh no, was I planning on things to do with Zachary? I thought I was going to ditch this kid. It was so hard to decide what I should do. Maybe I should try to talk to Zachary.

I do know how good it feels when someone spends time with you and listens to what you have to say. It's scary saying something out loud that has been private in your head, but it does feel good to get it out of there. It's kinda like cleaning up the dirty, sticky, messy, dead rodent stuff out of a kitchen. When you're done it just feels better, like there's a clean space to fill with new things. Maybe if Zachary would talk to me he could feel that too.

The Meeting

The more I thought about meeting with Zachary, the more worried I became. Maybe I could just sneak home and hide out there. When the lunch bell rang, I jumped up and quickly darted between kids leaving the classroom. I decided I would do my best to get out the front doors and home before I could be seen.

As I leapt down the stairs two at a time, I was met at the bottom by Mr. Lily and a scared looking little boy. Zachary looked much smaller than I had expected. He had short red hair and a thin little face covered in freckles. He held Mr. Lily's big hand with both of his tiny hands. He looked up at me and then down at his shoes. His big blue eyes looked red and puffy. Had he been crying? Now what? What do I do? Do I run past them and deal with the consequences later? Do I stop and meet this little guy? Mr. Lily decided for me. He reached out his arm and guided me gently to the side of the hall as I came off the last step.

"Well, hello Mr. Wilson," his voice boomed. "We have been waiting for you!" I always like Mr. Lily's voice. It is strong but kind at the same time.

Mr. Lily walked alongside Zachary and I to the empty gym. He introduced me to Zachary and told him I was one of his favorite students. Really? Zachary looked up at my face for a couple seconds, then went back to looking at his shoes. Mr. Lily took out some basketballs and said we could play in the gym while he went to get our lunches.

Okay, what do I do now? Zachary looked like he was going to cry, and I knew I was no good at dealing with a crying kid.

I dribbled the basketball for a little while, then called out, "Hey, catch!" as I threw the ball to Zachary. He didn't put his hands up and the ball hit him in the chest. He started to cry. I walked over to Zachary, put my arm around his shoulders and said, "Sorry buddy, you were supposed to catch that." He just cried harder, and ran and hid under the bleachers.

With a hysterical first grader, and not a clue about what I should do, I sat down on the floor and put my head in my hands. I remember hiding when things were just too much for me. I flashed back on a memory of hiding in the bathroom stall a couple years ago during science class. I had gotten angry when kids were teasing me because my pants were too short. (Was it my fault that I had a growth spurt?) I didn't want to get into any more trouble, but I felt like I was going to slug someone. I ran to the boy's bathroom, went in the stall, locked the door, and sat crouched with my feet on the toilet seat so no one could see my feet under the door. I stayed there through the whole science class. I just needed to be away from everyone. Mr. Williams, my teacher, must not have missed me, and when the bell rang at the end of class time, I walked out and felt stronger to go on with my day. Maybe I understood what Zachary was feeling right now.

I gave him time, and then finally asked Zachary to come and sit down. "Let's just roll the ball back and forth to each other." I said quietly. After a minute or so, Zachary did as I asked and we pushed the ball back and forth to each other in silence.

It seemed like forever before Mr. Lily came back with our lunches. When he did, he said we could go to the office and eat lunch with him which made me feel better. Maybe he'd know what to say to this fear-filled little guy.

On the way I tried, "I don't feel good and I better go home." but Mr. Lily didn't respond. He just kept talking about how good the hot lunch looked today.

When we got to Mr. Lily's office, he pushed two chairs up to his desk. Zachary scrambled up on one, his feet barely dangling off the edge. The chair was so big in comparison to him, it looked like he was a little doll sitting there. I sat in the other chair and Mr. Lily faced us across the desk.

Mr. Lily tried to begin a conversation by asking, "Well boys, when do you think we'll get our first snow this year?" I shrugged my shoulders and Zachary made humming noises as he gobbled up the food on his tray. I decided that eating was a good idea, as it wouldn't be polite to talk while I was eating. I took my cue from Zachary and started eating like I was starving. We all sat there shoveling mini corn dogs in our mouths without a word being said. When we finished, Mr. Lily brought out a dish of little candy bars he had hidden in his drawer. Zachary and I both grabbed for the candy like frog tongues snapping for a fly, and our hands hit each other.

Without thinking, we both started to laugh, which prompted Mr. Lily to chuckle. "Well, I think I've found something you boys have in common!"

As we were enjoying our candy, Zachary squeaked out in a tiny voice, "Tomorrow."

"What?" Mr. Lily asked.

"The snow. I think it's going to snow tomorrow." Evidently Mr. Lily thought that was the funniest thing he'd ever heard, and his laughter roared throughout the tiny office. We figured that must have been really funny, so Zachary and I decided to have a good laugh with him.

Old Friend, New Friend

I thought a lot about Zachary all afternoon. My body attended classes, but my mind replayed visions of him crying and hiding under the bleachers, those blue eyes encircled with red puffiness, and his tiny body sitting in that big padded chair in Mr. Lily's office. What a fragile little guy.

I wondered if others had ever looked at me and saw sadness like I see in Zachary. I know how hard he was going to have to work to get beyond that. You know, sometimes when you just focus on yourself you don't notice that others may be feeling stuff just like you. Our meeting did end with hearing Zachary laugh, and I felt encouraged that maybe we, Mr. Lily and I, would be able to help this little boy who needed us so very much. I decided I was glad to be helping Zachary.

All the fourth and fifth graders ended the day in the gym with a movie about the solar system. I guess they figured by Friday afternoon we couldn't focus anymore in class, or maybe the teachers just needed a break. We all crowded down the stairs, packed tightly together like a herd of cattle. We made a right turn at the bottom and headed towards the gym. As we went through those big gym doors, I looked to my left and there was Shawn. I was surprised that with all these kids, we were standing right next to each other. He smiled at me, and we continued to file up the bleacher steps. We sat next to each other at the end of the top row.

"Do you still have Max?" I asked. I don't usually talk to anyone at school, and it felt good to have someone I was comfortable with right next to me in this crowd of bodies.

"Yup, I do! You want to take him for a walk with me after school?"

"Yeah!" I answered. "Does he still like to run after squirrels?"

"He sure does! He also likes putting his nose into the leaves and pushing them down the sidewalk! It's the funniest thing!"

It was nice sitting next to someone I thought I could call my friend. The lights dimmed and the movie began. We watched the planets revolve around the sun, while intense music boomed throughout the gym. My body took the opportunity to relax and I let my mind go, imagining myself floating through the atmosphere, circling each planet and heading to the next one. I felt light and weightless, my eyes closing at times while the music seeped into my skin.

Before I was ready, the credits of the movie were scrolling down the screen and the harsh lights returned, making me cover my eyes with my arm to shield them from the brightness. Mr. Lily stood before us in the center of the gym. He dismissed us, and told us to have a great weekend.

Shawn and I walked together to our lockers to get our backpacks, and then to homeroom to end the day. When the bell rang, I stayed in my desk until Shawn reached me.

We walked out following the crowd through the halls, down the stairs, and out the front door. Warm sunshine greeted us as we entered the weekend.

We raced to the crosswalk and began laughing. Once we were allowed to cross, we continued down the sidewalks together, running in circles trying to escape armfuls of leaves we'd pick up and throw at each other. By the time we made it to the park we were laughing so hard we couldn't keep going. We flopped down in the grass, making a loud crunch in the leaves as our bodies hit the ground.

Looking up into a sky of cottony clouds, both of us spotted a cloud that looked like a Tyrannosaurus Rex! We watched as the breeze slowly distorted the dinosaur into a giant amoeba shaped blob. When the blob broke up into tiny amoebas that floated away, Shawn asked if I was ready to go and get Max. We got up and ran as fast as we could to Shawn's house.

As we turned the corner and came around the front yard of the house, Max was waiting for us! He was hooked to a chain and started yelping and jumping up in excitement the minute he saw us! Shawn unhooked the clasp from Max's collar, attached the leash, and we all took off down the driveway and back toward the park. As Max bounced along he kept turning his head back to look at us, giving us barks of gratitude. We gave it our best sprint, but we still couldn't go fast enough for him. He pulled on Shawn's arm, twisting his right shoulder forward, making Shawn look like he was running sideways!

Max stuck his nose in the crisp leaves, snuffling along the sidewalk just as Shawn said he would. Once we made it to the park, Shawn unhooked Max's leash. That crazy dog ran in circles around us, making us dizzy just watching him. He barked and shook his head and I wondered if he was happy to see me again! I found a stick and threw it across the field and Max sprinted to get it, almost getting to it before it hit the ground. He raced back to us, his ears flopping up and down. He dropped the stick on his owner's shoes, and Shawn took his turn flinging the stick as far as he could. Again, Max raced to get it and returned it to us.

We kept this up until Max was panting so hard he decided to take a break. Instead of bringing the stick back to us, he came close, sprawled out on the grass like a bear rug, and laid his head on top of the stick, protecting it so we could play again later! We took his cue and stretched out on the grass by him.

Feeling tired and happy, and once again studying the sky for cloud pictures, we were interrupted by a tiny woman in a fuzzy purple and green striped jogging suit. She wore bright orange tennis shoes, and a baseball cap that allowed just a little of her curly snow white hair to peek out.

"Enjoying this great day?" she asked.

"We sure are, Mrs. Halpa!" Shawn answered.

This colorful woman continued, "I have a job for you boys if you want it. I am looking for someone to come and rake. My yard is so full of leaves."

Shawn and I looked at each other and said, "Sure!" at exactly the same time.

"I will not only pay you with cold, hard, cash, but I will also add some fresh baked cookies to your wages! You can start tomorrow."

That sounded great and we agreed to meet tomorrow morning at 9:00 in her front yard.

"Zippity! That will be fantastic!" Mrs. Halpa exclaimed.

We watched her march back across the street and through her leaf-filled yard, pulling her knees up high, and swinging her arms rhythmically as she went. The leaves were up to her knees as she marched through them all the way to her front steps.

"Want to come home with me?" Shawn asked. "Mom works nights now, but she leaves me stuff for supper. We can eat and then watch a movie or something."

"Sounds good!" I answered as we stood up. Shawn clipped the leash back on Max's collar. We didn't bother running this time as we made our way down the sidewalks. I felt a nice kind of tired and it didn't seem to take long before we were at Shawn's front door. He pulled a chain holding his house key out from under his T-shirt. It looked uncomfortable as he bent forward far enough to get the key in the lock and turn it. He removed the key from the lock, tucked it back under his shirt, and pushed the door open.

Max rushed in alongside us and went right to his water bowl, lapping up all the water it contained. He dribbled on the floor, and then used his tongue to gather the last few droplets from his snout. Shawn refilled the bowl from the kitchen sink and I flopped down on the couch.

He read the note aloud that his mom had attached to the refrigerator. "Hi Shawn! There is just peanut butter and jelly for sandwiches tonight. I need to go grocery shopping. Have a good night! Love you, Mom."

"Sure hope you like peanut butter and jelly, Jack." Shawn giggled as he started taking out what we needed to make our sandwiches.

"Sounds good to me!" I answered, as I joined him in the kitchen. We each took 4 slices of bread which finished off the loaf, and smeared thick peanut butter over two slices. Grape jelly covered our other two pieces, and we placed all four slices together! We looked at each other, opened our mouths as wide as we could, then sunk our teeth into these masterpieces.

We automatically said, "Mmmmm," at the same time, and gave each other a closed mouth smile. I have to say that it tasted amazing!

Shawn went to the fridge and took out a jug of milk. He poured us each a big glass to help unstick our mouths. We finished our sandwiches in silence. I helped Shawn put everything away, and wipe off the counter that was speckled with our sticky sandwich ingredients.

Shawn turned the T.V. on, and we watched an old Spider-Man movie I had seen once before. It was as fun and exciting as watching it the first time. Shawn and I pretended to shoot webs out around the room from our wrists. We laughed until our stomachs hurt.

By the time the movie was finished it was dark outside, so I thought I'd better get home. Shawn and I double-checked our plans to meet at Mrs. Halpa's house tomorrow morning at 9:00, and I headed out. It had gotten pretty chilly since the sun had gone down, and I decided not to dawdle on my way home.

Alice welcomed me home by rubbing her body against my legs as I opened the front door. She purred loudly and gave me a squeaky meow. I have to say I was happy to see her and scooped her up into my arms, rubbing her fur against my cheek.

"Welcome home, girl!" I said aloud. I locked the door, closed the window I had left open for her, and ran up the stairs to my room. Alice jumped up on my bed, made a circle and waited for me to pet her. Sometimes it bothered me when she wanted so much attention, but tonight I was happy to see her, and we fell asleep snuggled together on the bed.

Work Never Felt So Good

I watched the chicken clock all morning and when it was finally 8:45, I raced out the front door and down the street. As I got close to Mrs. Halpa's house, I could see Shawn waving his arms and Max running around him in circles. I walked into the yard and bent down to rub Max's ears.

Mrs. Halpa opened the front door and came to greet us, an amazing aroma following her into the yard. She carried a big plate of chocolate chip cookies and told us we better eat some for energy! They were huge, still warm with gooey chocolate, and I thanked her with my mouth full, as I grabbed for my second cookie.

"The rakes are in the garage boys, and I will bring out some plastic bags for you to put the leaves in." She had such a big smile on her face. I guess it made her happy she wouldn't have to march through all these leaves after today. If I had a grandma, I would like her to be like Mrs. Halpa. She was always so happy, and she wore such fun, crazy clothes. Today was a long black skirt that had tall golden giraffes all around it. With those bright orange tennis shoes peeking out underneath her skirt, it made it look like the giraffes were wearing them! What was best about Mrs. Halpa, was she had a big heart. She cared about you even if she didn't know your name or how not-normal your life was. I felt good about helping this delightful lady!

I finished my second cookie, grabbed one more and headed to the garage. Shawn and I each found a rake and went to the front yard. Starting on opposite sides, we raked the leaves to one huge pile in the middle. Grandma H. as I decided I would call her in my head, was right. There were a LOT of leaves in her yard. It wasn't easy trying to round them up into one spot with Max racing through them every time we got a good pile started! We got the bags and started filling them, deciding that the less leaves Max had to spread around as we worked, the better. We did well as a team. Shawn held the bags open while I shoved leaves in as fast as I could. After we had filled six big bags, we sat down on the front steps to take a break.

Grandma H. must have seen us sit down and she rushed out the front door with two glasses of ice cold lemonade for us, and a bowl of water for Max. It was a cool, crisp day, but with all the work we were doing our bodies felt warm and sweaty.

"Zippity! You boys are doing great!" she squealed. We chatted for a few minutes and then she returned inside.

"I like this lady!" I told Shawn, "How do you know her?"

"She's a friend of my mom, and she used to babysit me." Shawn shared. "She is the nicest person I know, but her fashion sense.....well, you know!" We chuckled and finished our lemonade. I was starting to feel tired, but I wasn't going to let this lady down. We gave each other a look as if to say, let's do this, and went back to raking.

We had the whole front yard done when Grandma H. brought out a colorful quilt and spread it on the flattest part of the yard. She went back inside and carried out a picnic basket that she set on the quilt. As she was removing our lunch from the basket, we went inside to wash up. Walking into her house we were met by lemon colored walls. She had brightly colored paintings all over the walls, and at first glance it just made a person feel happy. We washed our hands and headed back outside. All three of us sat together and enjoyed turkey sandwiches, along with chips, pickles, and something she called Mandarin Orange Salad. Of course there were more cookies for dessert.

We shared stories and Gran (what I was NOW calling her in my head), had some of the best stories I had ever heard. She made us laugh so hard, once making milk squirt out my nose! As we sat enjoying this time, Gran got up and skipped around while holding up the tennis shoe wearing giraffes! I guess she was happy to have a leaf-free yard!

The backyard was smaller than the front, and we finished raking it in no time at all. After bagging up the rest of the leaves, we placed a total of 12 bags in Gran's driveway. We put the rakes back in the garage and went up to the door.

"All done?" Gran sang through the screen door. She came out holding a handful of bills. "Here you go boys. Thanks so much for your help. You split this money up between yourselves, okay?"

"Thanks Gran, I mean, Mrs. Halpa!" I corrected myself quickly, feeling foolish for calling her Gran out loud.

She smiled her big smile and continued, "I had three calls today from neighbors who wanted to know who the hard working boys in my yard were, and if you could rake their lawns. I gave them your phone number Shawn. It looks like you guys are now in the leaf raking business!" We thanked Gran for the money, and the good food. She told us to come over anytime we wanted. Before we left, Mrs. Halpa bent down and whispered in my ear, "You can call me Gran anytime you want!"

We stayed busy with our raking jobs for the next couple weeks, often working after school as well as on the weekends. Almost every person we worked for gave us names of other friends that wanted our help. When we had raked almost every lawn in a couple block radius, the snow started, and we realized our raking business was over for this year.

I put all my earnings in a quart jar and Shawn used a Ziplock bag. We sat down together on a Saturday afternoon and decided to count our big bucks. Once we had counted out all the money, we found we each had earned $100. Wow! That felt great! Even though we hadn't spent any money yet, it felt good to have it, just in case we needed it. We talked about what we might spend our money on, and our ideas got crazier as we kept going! I finally decided I would order pizzas to be delivered to my house every day for a whole week, each night trying a different kind. Shawn said that he would buy a chess set made out of chocolate, so he could eat all the pieces when he was done playing the game! It sure felt good to have a friend to act crazy with!

Doing What Friends Do

It turned out that almost all the people we raked leaves for turned into snow shoveling customers. I guess everyone thought we did a good job. After shoveling snow for three people after school today, I came home and flopped down on my bed. My arms were so tired that I could hardly lift them up. It only took about a minute before Alice joined me and I pet her while her motor purred. It had been a long day as usual, but I felt content as well as exhausted.

My life had been so different the past few weeks. I was thankful that things were better than they used to be. I felt different now and I liked it. I guess that's why it's good to have people in your life. Not only does it feel good to have someone there for you, like Shawn and Gran, but it also feels good to be the one there for someone else. Zachary had shown me that for sure. When I help him, it makes me feel like, I don't know, like I got up in the morning for a reason. Before, all I worried about was me and I guess sometimes I still do, but there's more to me now.

Things have gotten better with Zachary since that first day we met. I look forward to seeing him each day, and he doesn't look at his feet anymore when we're together. He looks me right in the eyes like he's trying to read my mind. We eat lunch away from the others in my class, but I don't worry about being seen with Zachary anymore. Mr. Lily stops once in a while to talk to us, and he never forgets to leave us candy. Shawn joins us sometimes too. Zachary talks a lot now, and is always asking me questions.

Most of the time, we just talk about dinosaurs. Who knew he was a dinosaur lover? I used to love them too when I was smaller, but somehow I had forgotten about how much I enjoyed learning about them. If we eat fast, we go to the library and look at dinosaurs in books and on the computer with the rest of our time. It's weird you know, that we have the same interest even when we're so far apart in age. I brought in some dinosaur models that I found in the corner of my closet under old clothes that don't fit me anymore. I used to sleep with those models when I was little. I told Zachary he could take them home for a while if he wanted to. I thought he was going to cry when I told him that - not in a sad way, but in a way I knew he appreciated me letting him do that.

Sometimes when I've seen Zachary in the hall, he still has a sad look on his face. He smiles when we are together though, and he looks like a different kid than the day he stood at the bottom of the stairs waiting for me with Mr. Lily. It makes me wonder what has made him so sad. I want to ask him someday, but not yet. I don't want him going back to looking at his shoes when we're together. I know it's hard to say some things out loud. I get that.

I hope Mr. Lily keeps letting us have our lunches together. I have to admit I like having a "little buddy." I can't believe I was so scared when Mr. Lily first asked me about helping Zachary. I didn't think that I could do a good job, but I know that we are both happy when we are together, especially when we are talking about dinosaurs.

Mr. Lily stopped me in the hall the other day and said Zachary's mom, his adopted mom, called to say Zachary has been talking a lot about me at home, and that he has seemed happier. Mr. Lily said that his teacher has noticed him trying more things in the classroom too, and he has been crying less.

"I just wanted to let you know that it is because of you, Jack. You have made a positive difference in the life of this young boy. You should feel very proud." Wow, that made me feel good! I didn't know how to answer Mr. Lily, but I gave him a big smile. I know he's happy when we are together, but I was glad to hear that even when we aren't together, Zachary is doing better.

Every Wednesday since we raked at Gran's house, we stop to see if she has any jobs we can help her with. That's what friends do for each other. I call her Gran out loud all the time now, and not just in my head. I think she likes that because it always puts a big smile on her face!

I love going to Gran's house. It smells deliciously like whatever she's been baking that day, and we get to sample what she's made. We talk about school, and she tells us about new exercises they are doing in her water aerobics class. She has a card table set up in her living room with a 5,000 piece jigsaw puzzle of exotic animals. We try to help her find a few pieces while we talk and laugh. I think it's going to take her a whole year to finish this new puzzle, with all those little pieces. Shawn and I always guess what color outfit she will be wearing before we get there. Last week she looked kinda like a parrot with a lime green jumpsuit thingy, and a bright orange scarf on her head. It makes me smile every time I think about how she looked that day!

Shawn and I walk to school in the morning, and walk home together after school. I have now been to school ON TIME for 10 days in a row! Mr. Lily says he just can't believe it! I try hard to be ready when Shawn gets to my house. After school we do our homework together right away before we do anything else. Shawn is really good at math and he helps me with tricky fraction problems I can't figure out, (We've moved to dividing fractions now, just when I was getting the hang of multiplying them), and I help him with his writing journal. He says he never can think of things to write about. I have hundreds of ideas in my head, so I have plenty to share with him.

Shawn talks about missing his mom because she's at work a lot. At least he gets to see her on Sundays, and they usually do something fun together. Last Sunday, Shawn said they went sledding, then had hot chocolate and played chess when they got home. (Not with chocolate chess pieces, of course!) He said he won fair and square three times! It made me happy that they had such a fun day together.

Shawn sometimes talks about what it was like to be in foster care. He looks really sad when he starts talking about that. He didn't like being away from his mom, and he hopes that he won't have to go back. It sounded like his foster parents were nice enough, but it was different there, and it was hard for Shawn to get used to. I hope he doesn't have to go back too. I would really miss him this time.

Shawn and I have gotten good at talking to each other. I wasn't used to doing much talking, and at first it felt kinda weird, but now sometimes we can't STOP talking! It feels good to be able to talk about important stuff, or even nothing important at all. I have wanted to talk to Shawn about my mom, but I've been afraid it will make it all too real if I say it out loud. It's one of those things that I've tried not to think about. It doesn't even make me that mad anymore. I guess I have decided this is how it's going to be for me. When I'm ready, I want Shawn to be the one I tell everything to.

The truth is, I haven't seen my mom since I asked her about getting a new alarm clock. I wonder if that upset her, and that is why she left for so long this time. I should probably tell someone, but then they're going to wonder why I didn't say something earlier. I used to think that each day when I got home from school she would be there. I don't think that anymore. I wish Miss Lor was still at school. She would know how to help me through this. I am used to being responsible for myself now, and I try to make the best out of every day. I still miss seeing my mom, even though she didn't talk to me very much when she was around. It was nice having her in the house though.

All Because of a Snowstorm

When I got up this morning it was so white outside, I could hardly see the street from my bedroom window. The wind was blowing and swirling the snow around. Oh boy, there will be lots of shoveling jobs today after school. I put my coat on over my pajamas, pulled on my boots and went out to shovel off the steps and the front sidewalk. The snow was wet and packed together. It was heavy when I'd throw each shovelful into the yard.

I finished the steps and had about half of the sidewalk shoveled when I heard, "Hey, Jack!" I turned around to see Shawn behind me. He had the biggest grin on his face. "Guess what? Did you hear? School is cancelled because of all this snow, and we're supposed to get a lot more! We have all day to get our shoveling jobs done!"

"What?" I could hardly believe it! "That is amazing! Come on inside so I can get ready!" As Shawn and I went up the steps, there was a layer of snow covering what I had already cleaned off. We got inside and took off our wet coats, hats, and boots, leaving them on the floor by the front door.

"I haven't eaten breakfast yet, or even gotten out of my pajamas!" I laughed, "Do you want something to eat?" I had picked out a box of Frosted Flakes, my favorite, and a jug of milk at the gas station yesterday, so I knew there would be enough for both of us.

"Sounds good!" Shawn answered. "I haven't had breakfast yet either." He sat down at the table while I got out bowls, spoons, and glasses. We sat there eating, with only the sound of crunching flakes being heard in the room.

Shawn interrupted the crunching. "Hey, Jack, I have been wanting to ask you something for a long time. How come I never see your mom or dad around? Do they work a lot too, like my mom?"

Whoa, I had not expected this right now. Is this the time I tell Shawn everything, or do I push it off as no big deal and move on? I shrugged my shoulders and kept eating.

"It's just that, well, I've been wondering." he continued.

"Well, I don't know my dad. He has never been around. It's only been my mom and me for as long as I can remember." I stopped talking and started eating my cereal again, thinking maybe that would be enough information to keep Shawn happy for now.

He continued, "Okay, but where's your mom? I've never seen her and I've been at your house a lot."

"It's kind of a secret. I don't want anyone to know." I answered, feeling my eyes shift down towards the floor. "My life is really not very normal." Shawn put his spoon down, folded his arms on the table, then looked right into my eyes.

"Okay, I'm ready," he said.

I knew now was the time. "I'm not sure where to start, but right now I don't know WHERE my mom is. She has been gone for weeks this time. She goes away a lot, but usually only for a few days at a time. She has never talked to me much, and I know there is something wrong, but I don't know what it is. She never says where she has been or why she left. I tried asking her so many times but it seemed to upset her. She would just walk away from me and go to her bedroom for hours. I stopped asking, thinking I wanted to keep her happy. This last time I asked her if I could get a new alarm clock, and I wonder if that made her mad enough to stay away longer." I stopped talking, and Shawn continued to quietly look into my eyes. "I don't know what to do." I told him.

It was getting harder to get my words out now, as I realized what I had actually said out loud. I had lived this way for so long, but when those words came out of my mouth and into the room where another person could hear them, I realized how horrible it all sounded. I could start to feel myself getting angry. I had pushed all this information back to a remote section of my brain that kept it hidden and secret. I had stopped feeling the anger that caused me to erupt in the past. Not thinking about it had helped me to keep going everyday.

I tried to continue, "Why doesn't....my mom.....care about me?"

Then I lost it. The tears came and I couldn't stop them. I took my cereal bowl and threw it on the floor. It made a louder sound than I had expected as it shattered into a million pieces throughout the kitchen. I kicked the chair over, then turned around, bent over the edge of the sink and cried like crazy. I didn't want Shawn to see me like this and I just stayed with my back towards him, sobbing until I could hardly catch my breath. I started using my breathing exercises, and finally my sobs lessened. I took a full breath.

Shawn hadn't made a sound this whole time, and I began to wonder if he was still there. I turned around and saw that he was still sitting in the same exact position at the table with his arms folded, and there were tears rolling down his face. He cried without making a sound while he let me get myself back under control.

I picked up the chair, set it back at the table and sat down. I put my hands over my face and held my head. You'd expect it to feel lighter after expelling all that information, but instead my head felt like it weighed more than my body. It ached and felt full, like it had expanded now that it was jam-packed with the truth. We sat there separately together with our tears and our feelings, wondering what we were supposed to do now.

Mr. Lily

Looking Back

I wanted to be a teacher. I remember when my friends were looking at colleges to become engineers, lawyers, and doctors, I knew the only job I wanted was to work with kids, and to help guide them in the right direction. Some thought it was an odd occupation for me to go into, but when I was in school, I was one of those kids who often chose the wrong path. In fact, I made some pretty bad choices at times.

I was lucky to have a fourth grade teacher who helped me see things differently. I also had good friends. They were more like brothers than just friends. My home life was difficult. No one wanted to go to my house after school, including me. Instead I went from school to houses that felt like homes. There would be snacks, reminders to do homework, a sit down supper with conversation, laughing, and getting along. I would wait there until it was close to bedtime before I'd head home and slip in quietly through the basement door. If I was lucky, no one would hear me.

The academic part of school was easy for me. I caught onto things pretty fast, and always had a good memory for details. That memory helped me with taking tests and I was usually one of the top students in the class each year. It was the getting along with others part of school that got me into trouble.

In my house we didn't really get along. I knew my parents loved me, but they just didn't know how to deal well with things that came up. They were quick tempered, and had trouble working out disagreements calmly. I guess that's why I never learned how to solve problems without getting upset. I wouldn't think before I'd act, and that was always a bad idea. At school when something happened that I didn't like, I would get upset, do crazy things, and end up in the principal's office. I would have to stay there until I was able to calm down. Sometimes that took me a long time. Looking back, I was lucky the principal gave me the time I needed to get myself under control.

By the time I got to fourth grade, I had started to figure out how to stay out of situations that got me into trouble. I also had a teacher that made a real difference. Mrs. Worthington treated me like I was her favorite student. Actually I think she treated everyone that way, but it still felt good.

She would give us projects where we would have to work together in groups and get along. When we were having trouble getting along, Mrs. Worthington would teach us strategies that helped us solve the problem and be able to share our ideas without getting upset with each other. She helped me start a new way of handling situations when I didn't agree with someone. It made me learn to listen to what everyone else thought, and to share my ideas calmly. She also taught us how to compromise when we just couldn't come to an agreement.

I started loving the times when we met in groups and I took pride in making sure our group got along. When others had trouble, I turned out to be the one that helped them work it out and have fun. I started feeling really good about that. I guess Mrs. Worthington saw that too, because one day she said she noticed how well I worked with others. She said that was a sign of a good leader.

I never forgot that moment, and how it felt. It was the first time someone told me I was good at something. I had never thought much about helping others. I usually just worried about me, and trying to keep myself under control. I decided that day, helping others felt good. I thought maybe I could work with kids and help them feel like Mrs. Worthington had made me feel.

Coming Up With a Plan

This is my first year at being assistant principal. Before that, I taught fifth grade. I loved teaching, but when the job posting for assistant principal came up, I just knew I would have to apply for it. As assistant principal, one of your main jobs is to deal with students that have behavioral problems. That had been me - student with behavioral problems. When I was teaching, I saw so many kids that reminded me of myself when I was their age.

I thought if I could focus my time on those kids, that would be perfect for me. So I applied for the job, and here I am the assistant principal at Pine Hills. What I didn't think about though, was how hard this was going to be.

You see, I care so much about these kids. I have to confess that I have a soft heart. I notice and feel what others are going through. When you feel so deeply about something, it is part of who you are. It's not like you can shut it off. I not only think about students during the school day, but also while I'm driving to school, on my way home, and I wake up in the night worrying about students. It's been a busy start to this school year, and I hope I get better at my job. Sometimes when I do something that works smoothly I think I have it all figured out, but then I make a mistake and I realize I have a lot to learn.

There's this one student, Jack Wilson. I have been watching him for awhile. I remember his mom from when

I was in high school. She was a couple years younger than me. She was so timid and shy that I don't think she ever spoke out loud at school. I never saw her with friends. She was always sitting by herself at lunch or in the library during study halls, looking sad.

Jack has had a lot of problems with being angry in the past. Although I am happy about his improvement in behavior, I also sense that there is something that's not right. I have been trying to figure it out, and I have to say he is one student I spend time thinking about. He seems as fragile as a sketch on paper, crumpled and shuffled throughout the school never really being seen. Jack is adept at being invisible within the halls of hundreds of other students. If I watch closely, I can catch glimpses of him, but he weaves in and out throughout the interactions of his classmates, never really noticed or involved in the freedom of childhood.

Jack talks to me more now, and he even looks directly at me. Whether we have connected beyond that eye contact, I'm unsure. We usually "bump into each other," in the morning. About the time the bell rings, he comes flying in the front doors like he's finishing the 100 yard dash. He's so out of breath, and I can usually just get him to slow down by walking alongside him to his classroom. I don't need him flying through the halls at that speed and taking out anyone in his way. It's not a great time to have much of a conversation though. We usually walk without speaking much, as he catches his breath and regains his composure.

Jack usually looks pretty disheveled and I wonder what his life is like at home. When I have left messages for his mom, I haven't gotten any responses. His grades have been pretty good and he reminds me a little bit of myself when I was his age. I won't give up on Jack, but I hope that I can figure out how to make a positive difference in his life.

Then there's a new student, Zachary, that arrived a few weeks ago. He was just adopted, and has been having a hard time getting used to a new home and a new school. I don't know all the details, but he has had some hard times. He cries a lot at school, and I just want him to know he can feel safe and happy here. It's like he has built a wall around himself and is afraid to trust anyone.

When he's in the classroom he doesn't interact with his classmates, and still won't talk to his teacher. I know that it takes time for some kids to feel comfortable, but it hurts me to think Zachary comes to school each day feeling the way he does.

As I have been wracking my brain to figure out what I can do to help this little guy, I had this brainstorm. What if providing opportunities for Jack and Zachary to interact would somehow benefit them both. Maybe Jack would feel good about helping someone, and Zachary could possibly connect to Jack as a person he could trust. I think it's worth a try.

A Good Start

I decided to look up Jack's address and pay him a visit at home one night after school. As I walked through the neighborhoods, it made me think of how I would visit my friends' houses after school when I was Jack's age. The streets lined with cracker box houses were close enough to each other that if neighbors reached out their side windows, they could shake hands! Narrow front yards stretched together to make a long rectangle of grass down the block, edged by a skinny sidewalk full of cracks just waiting to be stepped over. Suddenly I remembered myself being ten years old again, playing catch or Capture the Flag with Ben, Alan, and Joseph. We'd run through everyone's yards like they were a long football field.

I hadn't spoken to those guys in awhile, and I decided to make phone calls this weekend to catch up. I was the only one that stayed in Pine Hills, and the rest of my friends traveled to other states to live and work. Those families, those friends, those homes, made such a difference in my life when I was young. I never want to take them for granted, and I decided I needed to remind them how grateful I still am for their kindness.

When I spotted Jack's house, I walked along the sidewalk across the street for a while. I noticed that his house looked like it could use a little attention. It was in need of a new paint job and a couple of the windows were cracked. As I was looking at the broken concrete steps going up to the porch, I noticed an orange cat curled up, warming itself in the early evening rays of the sun.

I walked up the steps, and the cat leapt down and ran across the yard. It looked skinny and I wondered if it lived here, or had just stopped to bask in a sunny spot for awhile. I knocked on the front door and waited. I couldn't hear any sound from the house, and when I peeked in the window at the top of the door I didn't see any movement. I waited a bit, but then decided I hadn't picked the right time to find someone home. As I was being careful to walk down the broken steps, I heard Jack and turned around to see him looking through the screen door.

I peered into the entryway of the house to see if I could see Jack's mom. Just as I was going to ask Jack if she was home, he joined me out on the porch. Jack seemed nervous and thinking about it now, I guess I did most of the talking. I hoped he was going to like my idea.

As I explained my plan to him, I thought Jack may have been recalling some tough memories himself. His reaction only made me think that this relationship could be as beneficial to Jack as it could be to Zachary. I had this feeling that Jack would know how to provide Zachary, a child so unsure of himself, with what he needed to move beyond his fears.

The next morning I watched for Jack, but he wasn't anywhere to be found as the first bell of the school day rang. I waited for awhile after the bell and even walked outside to look down the street. I hoped I hadn't asked too much of him and he had decided to skip school. I walked up to room 210 to let Ms. Franklin know Jack was absent, and was shocked to see him sitting in his desk as other students were filing in the classroom. I let him know that he could meet Zachary at lunch today. I didn't want to wait too long to get things started with the boys.

Zachary's day hadn't started out so well. He had thrown his crayons and scissors during an art project and then crawled under a table in the back of the classroom, where he stayed for most of the morning. When his teacher asked him to come out and sit at the table with his classmates, he had screamed and cried. He didn't even want to go outside for recess, something that most kids never want to miss.

When I went to pick Zachary up to meet Jack for lunch, I wasn't sure if he was going to come with me. I explained that we were going to go meet his "big buddy" and I guess he decided that was okay.

During that first meeting, I can't say that things went very smoothly. Just when I was wondering if this had been a good idea, both boys grabbed for candy bars at the same time and their hands hit together. That caused them both to start laughing, and I have to say I started laughing too. Not that it was a big deal, but it seemed to "break the ice" a bit and that was the first time I had seen EITHER boy smile or laugh. After that they seemed a little more relaxed, and I heard Zachary speak for the first time since he'd been at school! I had a feeling that somehow this was all going to turn out okay.

Things Are Looking Up

I have to say that things have been going pretty well with Zachary and Jack. I have listened to many of their conversations at the door during lunch, and it is fantastic that they both have opened up and connected. Dinosaurs turned out to be a common factor between those two. I have tried to let them interact on their own as long as things have been going well, and have always remembered to bring them candy as a special treat!

I was so pleased when Zachary's teacher and mom had seen an improvement in his behavior. He was finally starting to feel comfortable, and I hoped it was only going to keep improving!

It appeared that Jack was showing improvement as well. He did seem a lot happier at school, and he had been getting to school on time lately, which I considered a miracle! His teachers said he had been turning his homework in on time, as well.

I tried calling Jack's mom to let her know how proud I was of him, and what a difference he had made for this young boy. The phone number we had in our files said this was not a working number, so I wondered what had happened there. I asked Jack if he could give me his mom's new phone number and he said he would check on it. When the permission slips went home for our upcoming field trip Jack said he lost it twice, and when he finally brought the third one back it had an unrecognizable signature. I gave him the benefit of the doubt, but now I am beginning to wonder.

Shawn

Rough Patches

I am so happy to be back in Pine Hills. I didn't know how much I liked it here until I wasn't here anymore. I was taken to Bay City, an unfamiliar place where it never felt comfortable or like home. I realized the truth about what Dorothy said in the *Wizard of Oz,* there being, "no place like home." No one asked me if I was okay with being moved. Just one day I am living at home in Pine Hills and the next day I am plucked from my home and placed into another. It was like an eagle swept down and captured me in it's mighty talons, then dangled me in the air until a place was found to discard me. Maybe I am being a little dramatic here, but that is how I felt. I know they told me it was in my best interest, and I understand that sometimes you don't get a choice. It's just hard having things happen to you that you can't control.

I think that happens to kids a lot. We are young and are just expected to adapt to whatever happens to us. At least someone should ask us what we're thinking, and take the time to listen to what we have to say. I have important thoughts in my head, even though I'm just a kid.

I guess that's why I appreciate being back in Pine Hills where my life is familiar and predictable, and I am back with my mom. I hope when I grow, up this part of my life somehow is erased from my memory and the good parts are what I remember. I have a feeling that isn't going to happen, but maybe......

My dad died about a year ago. Mom and I really miss him. One day he was eating breakfast with me before school, and when I got home that night I found out he was gone forever. It was a snowy morning and the roads were slippery. He got hit by a semi that jackknifed in the middle of the highway and died instantly, at least that's what they said.

If I had known that breakfast was the last time I was going to see him, I would have paid more attention. I would have told him I loved him before I left for school instead of saying, "See ya." I would have hugged him hard and breathed in that crazy aftershave he liked to wear on work days. I would have studied every detail of his face: the wrinkles that appeared around his eyes when he smiled, those funny dimples, his straight white teeth, burning it all into my memory to recall whenever I needed him. I know we have pictures, but sometimes it's important to be able to "see" someone right at that moment when you need them. Closing my eyes to see my father's face, has helped me through a lot of what Mrs. Halpa would call, "rough patches." She always says if we can just find things to help us get through the rough patches, then we can go onto "smooth sailing," for awhile.

Mrs. Halpa took care of us after the accident, both Mom and I. I stayed with her sometimes, and sometimes she came to our house. My mom was missing my dad a lot, and Mrs. Halpa knew it. She just stepped in and became part of our family. My mom stayed real sad and depressed, and it just got worse instead of better. It was hard for her to get out of bed and do things she needed to do as an adult and as a parent. Mrs. Halpa finally said she needed to go to a doctor and that is when it all happened.

My mom was put in a residential treatment facility that helps people with severe depression, and I was sent to foster care. You see, both mom and dad were only children, and my grandparents had been gone for a long time. I guess they usually try to place you with a relative first. They wouldn't let me stay with Mrs. Halpa because we weren't related and she wasn't a licensed foster home. That's when the eagle came swooping in to take me away.

It was all very frightening. Mrs. Halpa tried to keep me but was told that didn't follow the rules. So I was removed, "for my own good," and had to say goodbye to my mom, and Mrs. Halpa. I wrote to Mom all the time, and once she started feeling better she wrote back. That first letter I got from her was like ten Christmas presents all wrapped together! I was so happy to hear that she was finally out of bed and starting to do normal things again. When she was able to go home, I had to wait to see if she was going to do okay before I was allowed to go home. The day I finally went home was the best day of my life!

Back Home

Things have been pretty good since I've been back home. Mom still has to work a lot to make sure we have enough money. She said Dad didn't have any life insurance and things would be hard for awhile until we, "got back on our feet." I've been helping to make money by raking leaves and shoveling snow. Even though it's not tons of money, she says it really helps and she is proud of me. It hasn't even seemed like work because Jack and I have been doing our jobs together. We knew each other a little bit before I left, but now we spend lots of time together. It's like having a brother, except maybe we get along better than brothers would.

Jack and I have been going to Mrs. Halpa's house every week, and she is such a funny lady! Jack has adopted her as his grandma and she thinks that is pretty awesome! We love going there. Sometimes we help her and sometimes she helps us. She can make us laugh and puts us in a good mood. She's easy to talk to and really listens to what we say. She asks us questions and is interested in our answers. Sometimes we can sit together and say nothing at all, like when we are working on her crazy jigsaw puzzles. We get all focused on finding places for those tiny pieces to fit and before you know it, it's an hour later! Either way, talking or not talking, Jack and I like spending time at her house. She almost always has something delicious coming out of the oven when we get there. The smell in her kitchen is amazing, and whatever she makes tastes like it's come out of a restaurant, only better!

I have been having some important thoughts about Jack. None that I have shared with anyone, but I think about doing that. We spend most days together and I have never seen his parents, even when we've been at his house for hours. Jack uses his raking and shoveling money to buy things like food from the gas station, and mittens from the thrift store. Things I think a mom should buy. He never says anything about his parents and I have been so tempted to ask him, but I guess I'm afraid. I know that he used to get mad a lot, and I wonder if bringing up that subject would get him upset. I don't want to do that to my best friend. I will have to think more about what I should do.

I guess you could say I am worried Jack doesn't have what a kid needs. I don't mean toys, a cell phone, or things like that, but things like healthy food, warm clothes, hugs, and someone to watch over you. The important stuff, you know? I don't see my mom as much as I'd like to, but I know she loves me and is doing what she needs to take care of me. When I do get to spend time with her, she gives me SO many hugs, some for the days she missed seeing me the past week, and some to bank for the next week too! She makes sure there is food for me, and that I have clean clothes that fit me. I know working long hours six days a week is hard for her too, but we will get through this together.

The Words Are Out

When I finally asked the big question, I got an answer I don't know what to do with. Last week we had this big snowstorm and school was cancelled. You'd think that would be a wonderful thing, right? Well I thought so too, at first. I raced over to Jack's house to let him know, because his T.V. doesn't work and I didn't know how else he would find out the good news.

That crazy kid was outside shoveling in his pajamas when I got there, and he was as excited as I was when he heard the news! We went inside to have breakfast and talk about how we would plan our free day. That's when I got brave enough to ask him about his mom. I figured we had lots of time, and being in his own house without anyone around maybe he'd be more comfortable talking about it.

I could tell he didn't want to talk about it at first. It looked like he thought if he kept eating his cereal, I would forget about getting an answer to my question. When he finally started to talk to me about his mom, you could tell that it was hard for him to pull out those bad memories. It was like a volcano starting to simmer and then erupting with a fiery vengeance. I think he just wanted to tell me the facts at first, but then his feelings got all involved and it looked like his guts were being torn out. I didn't know what to do. I wanted to show him that I was listening so I braced myself at the table, looked straight at him and didn't move, not even my eyes. It hurt to hear what he had to say and I couldn't keep my tears from coming, but I refused to move. He deserved to have his friend truly listen to everything he was able to get out. I wanted to run out of the house and down the street to Mrs. Halpa, telling her that Jack needed help and I didn't know what to do. Instead I pushed my feet into the floor and stayed steady, for Jack, for my best friend. After Jack was calm we sat together not speaking, but feeling the words that had been spewed into the air. What were we going to do with the information that was now out there? I don't think either of us had a clue.

Jack

After All the Words

I am so thankful to have Shawn as my friend. He listened and HEARD everything I said. He didn't interrupt me or give me his opinion. Even after I calmed myself and sat down in silence at the table with Shawn, he continued to look right at me. He showed me he was ready to listen to anything else I needed to say. I wanted him to know how much it meant that he not only had asked the hard question, but stayed with me through the pain of letting those words escape from the vault where they had been stored. The words thank you didn't seem like enough, and I was too tired just then to find any more words to say. I finally gave Shawn a small smile, and he smiled back through the lines of dried tears.

"We'd better get at our shoveling jobs, or we're going to get fired." I tried to joke. Shawn nodded his head. I raced upstairs, got dressed, and then we were off through the snow covered neighborhood.

My body felt weak, as if getting all those words and feelings out had been the most strenuous exercise of my life. As we trudged down the sidewalk making silent footprints in the wet, heavy snow, I wondered how I was going to do the work ahead of me. My arms and legs felt like wobbly jello, and my head ached. I was glad I had Shawn walking this path with me today.

Once we started shoveling I felt better, and we got three driveways shoveled before noon. Next, we walked to Gran's house to shovel for her, and she shouted for us to come inside. She had us put our wet coats, mittens, and hats in her dryer to get them ready for our next jobs.

There was a wonderful smelling lunch all ready to be eaten, spaghetti and meatballs with garlic bread. We helped Gran set the table and sat down while she brought over the food. While we were eating she studied our faces, as if she knew something was wrong. Maybe it was our red puffy eyes or our subdued excitement over a snow day that gave us away, but she didn't press us for any information. I imagined her rewinding and watching the film of what we had been through today. What would she think? We chatted politely about the snow, that she was almost done with the hardest puzzle she had ever done, and small things that kept our minds busy from any serious thought.

In this brightly colored home, with this uniquely dressed adopted grandmother, I felt comfortable and content. I didn't have to be strong or scared here, I could just be. We stayed longer than we probably should have, knowing how much more work we had left, but I hated to leave.

Gran gave us bags of oatmeal raisin cookies to tuck into our coat pockets for later, and we thanked her for an amazing lunch. We shoveled for Gran and two other customers, then headed to Shawn's house. Max was happy to see us. He raced out the front door and made trails through the snow in the front yard, celebrating the massive amount of white stuff we had gotten. The heavy snow had stopped now, and just a few feathery flakes floated from the dark clouds.

After Max was ready to come back in the house, we flopped down on the couch in the living room. Shawn and I devoured the bags of delicious cookies. We covered up with furry blankets that were on the couch, closed our eyes and started reliving the events of the day. When I opened my eyes again, it was dark outside. I looked over at Shawn on the other end of the couch. His eyes were still closed. Max was sprawled out between us, his head on Shawn's legs. I kept still and quiet with my thoughts until Shawn started to stir.

"We must have worked hard or something." I spoke in a whisper.

Shawn grinned a small grin and opened one eye. "Wow, how long did we sleep?" he responded, as he opened the other eye and saw how dark it was outside.

Looking around the room I began, "Hey Shawn, I just wanted to...tell you..." I stopped to think about what words I would choose to convey how much I appreciated him listening to me this morning.

"Yup, I know....." he cut in. We looked at each other and smiled.

The last two days of the week, things went pretty much as usual. I kept thinking about what I had told Shawn and although we hadn't said anymore about it, I figured he was thinking about it too.

Mr. Lily had asked me again for my mom's phone number, and I made him think I had forgotten to ask her. I hated lying to Mr. Lily. I really liked him and knew he deserved the truth. I was just worried about what would happen if an adult knew my mom had been gone for almost two months now. She had never been gone this long before. There had been lots of bills coming in the mail now, and I wasn't sure what to do about them. I was happy to be making money with my raking and shoveling jobs, but I sure didn't make enough to pay for things like heat and lights in the house.

Not the Friday Night
I Expected

On our way home after school, I told Shawn I wanted to stop at the gas station and buy a frozen pizza for our supper. I had been eating a lot of suppers at his house, and I wanted to treat him to supper tonight. We spent a long time looking at all the kinds of pizzas in the huge freezer, and we finally decided on a large sausage and mushroom. Neither of us liked all the onions and green peppers that seemed to dot most of the pizzas we saw.

We walked to my house and put the pizza in the freezer. Shawn pulled out the chess set he kept in his backpack and we sat down on the living room floor to play a few games before supper. I was still learning the game and wasn't very good at it yet, so Shawn won most of the time. That's okay though. It was still fun, and I loved seeing how happy it made Shawn to play.

After we got done playing, we stretched out on the carpet and sighed, like those games of chess had worn us out! I was going to give myself a couple minutes and then I'd preheat the oven for the pizza. I know that you DO have to preheat the oven first, like the directions say. Last time I put a pizza in the oven, and THEN turned the oven on, the top of the pizza got burnt like black charcoal. I tried to eat it, but it tasted really bad.

While staring at the pebbled ceiling like it was the most interesting thing he'd ever seen, Shawn asked in a careful sounding voice, "When are we going to talk about the elephant in the room?"

I looked around the room, then sat up and faced him. "What elephant?"

"Haven't you ever heard someone say that when you needed to talk about something?" he continued.

I was totally confused now.

"I figured you might not know what I was talking about, so I looked it up and memorized what it meant. If you say there's an elephant in the room, *there is an obvious problem everyone is aware of, but no one wants to discuss.* My mom used that phrase on me when we needed to talk about stuff after my dad died, and neither of us wanted to. Do you get it?"

"Oh." was all I could get out. Why did Shawn think he could ruin our fun afternoon by bringing up the mom issue again? I had been thinking more about it and he probably had too, but right now I didn't want to talk about it.

Shawn charged on, "I'm worried about what's going to happen when someone finds out that you're living by yourself. They are going to put you in foster care like they did with me, and we may never see each other again. We need to think about a plan so that doesn't happen. I've been thinking about this a lot and I don't know what we can do, but maybe together we can figure out something."

Shawn made sense, but my first reaction was to be mad at him for making me talk about this painful stuff again. He really did care about me, so I decided to forgive him.

"And what about your mom? If she IS missing, don't you think someone should know so they can look for her? What if she's dead or something?"

Now we both were sitting up looking at each other with wide eyes. I'm embarrassed to say I hadn't thought of things that way. My mom was always leaving me, and I just thought she did that to punish me when I did something wrong. I figured she didn't like me much. Why would a mom leave her kid so he has to do everything for himself? Did she ever wonder if I had food to eat, a warm coat for the winter, or if I went to school? It was too much for me to think about sometimes. I couldn't imagine what would make her not care. Now Shawn was giving me a different perspective. Maybe there's another reason she hasn't come home.

"Okay, so where do we start?" I began.

Shawn countered with, "Haven't got a clue, but maybe there's someone we can ask. We could talk to Mr. Lily, but I think he has to report stuff like that. It's in his job description or something. Maybe we should go to the library and look up how to keep a kid from being put in foster care. Did you tell me you don't have any relatives?"

"Yeah, I don't know anyone that I'm related to except my mom."

Shawn got up and started rummaging through his backpack, finally pulling out a notebook and a pen.

He headed over to the kitchen table saying, "Let's brainstorm ideas like Ms. Franklin does when we do problem solving stuff."

I thought that was a good idea and I followed him into the kitchen. I turned the oven onto preheat. We were going to need some food to work on this "elephant." Shawn wrote a title on the top of the notebook page, *How to Save Jack*.

"We could do nothing and hope that my mom comes back soon." I began. Shawn looked at me, raising one eyebrow. "Put it down." I urged, "Ms. Franklin says when you brainstorm, you put down ALL ideas that you think of." Shawn obediently wrote down my first idea. We sat staring at the page while Shawn jiggled the pen in his fingers. "We could call Miss Lor." I added. "She probably has to report this stuff too, but put that down anyway." We kept coming up with ideas we realized probably wouldn't work, but we faithfully put them on the paper. Ms. Franklin would have been proud of us. The oven had beeped, so I put the pizza in and set the timer. When the timer rang telling us the pizza was done, we were happy to take a break.

I put on heavy oven mitts, carefully took the pizza out of the oven, and put it on the cutting board. It smelled great, but to be honest I had stopped feeling hungry about four ideas ago. I grabbed the metal wheelie pizza cutter and cut the pizza in half and then in fourths. I thought about leaving the pieces nice and big like that, but decided I'd better make one more cut in each of them. As I started cutting the pizza into eighths, the doorbell rang. I leaned back to glance at the door while the pizza wheel sliced deep into my pointer finger. The blood started squirting onto the pizza and I let out an enormous howl. I heard the screen door open and heavy footsteps rush into the kitchen.

"Jack, are you okay? I heard you scream, and...." Mr. Lily took one look at the blood gushing out of my finger, grabbed one of the oven mitts on the counter and pushed it on the cut to slow the bleeding. He had me sit down, held my hand up in the air, and directed Shawn to find a clean towel or shirt or something he could wrap around my finger. Shawn went running around looking in drawers and closets and came back with a white undershirt. Mr. Lily used his teeth to make a hole and then ripped a long strip of T-shirt off the bottom. He removed the oven mitt and the blood spurted all over his shirt. He used the piece of T-shirt to wrap tightly around my finger.

I was watching all this, and although it hurt like it was real, it seemed like I was in some kind of dream. All that blood, Mr. Lily in my kitchen, Shawn, who's face had now turned a pearly white - what was going on?

Mr. Lily sat down next to me, continuing to hold my hand up in the air.

"Sit down Shawn, it's okay." he directed. Shawn did as he was told, then put his head down on the table. Even though I felt like putting my head down on the table, I tried to stay upright. Just as Mr. Lily was saying, "Where's your mom, Jack?" I saw him glance towards the notebook of ideas to "Save Jack," lying in the middle of the table. I didn't have enough energy to reach out and grab it away, and Shawn hadn't noticed now that he had his eyes closed tight. I could see Mr. Lily's eyes scanning back and forth, reading the myriad of ideas we had brainstormed just minutes ago.

I was afraid of what he was going to say next, but all I heard was, "You're going to need stitches Jack. That cut looks really deep. Can I take you to the emergency room?" I wanted to say no, but I was feeling really weak, and seeing the blood soak through the make-shift T-shirt bandage was making my stomach feel queasy.

Mr. Lily tried again, "Is your mom home, Jack?" I shook my head no. "Is YOUR mom home, Shawn?" Shawn shook his head without opening his eyes. "Okay, I'm going to take both of you boys with me to the emergency room."

Mr. Lily guided us, one at a time into his back seat, pulled the seat belts out and buckled us in tight. He told Shawn to make sure I kept my hand up so it was above my heart. He said that would help to slow the bleeding. By the look on Shawn's face, he wasn't capable of helping in any way right now. We both rested our heads back on the seat, as Mr. Lily drove faster than I think he should have to the hospital emergency room. By that time, the blood dripping through the T-shirt bandage had made crimson colored polka dots on my jeans.

Mr. Lily looked worried when he opened the back car door to get me out. He glanced first at me and then at Shawn, helping me up and telling Shawn he'd be right back. Shawn didn't answer. I leaned on Mr. Lily as he guided me to the front desk and explained about my finger.

The lady behind the desk asked a lot of questions. I told her my name and address. I also gave her my mom's name. She said they needed to see an insurance card. Mr. Lily said we didn't have that information, but they should take care of me and he would pay the total bill with his credit card. They didn't want to take me without an insurance card, but Mr. Lily was very persuasive. I had to sit in a wheelchair, and a nurse came out and pushed me back towards a small cold room.

I saw Mr. Lily head for the door to get Shawn, while saying, "I'll be right back. You'll be fine." Mr. Lily parked the car, then escorted Shawn into the waiting area. He placed him in a chair in front of a T.V. to watch *Wheel of Fortune*, and assumed it was a safe place to leave him.

The nurse told me her name was Felicia, and had me sit down on a skinny, hard bed. She hooked me up to a blood pressure machine that made a loud humming noise, and squeezed my arm like it was a bully. She took my temperature running a smooth, shiny instrument across my forehead and down the side of my cheek.

I got asked dozens of questions, like how much I weighed, if I was allergic to anything, and whether I take any medication. I was supposed to describe in detail how I had gotten cut, and Felicia kept asking where my parents were. I didn't feel like answering any questions. Mr. Lily came into the room as Felicia was removing the piece of T-shirt that was wrapped around my finger. She asked who had wrapped up my finger, and Mr. Lily said that he had. She told him it had been a good idea to wrap the finger to place pressure on the wound to help it stop bleeding. Only it really hadn't stopped yet. Once unwrapped, the finger began spewing blood onto the bright white sheets.

I tried not to look. The nurse grabbed a roll of white gauze, and once again began wrapping my finger tightly.

Mr. Lily came alongside the bed and put his hand on my shoulder, softly saying, "Everything is going to be okay, Jack. Everything is going to be okay."

A Long Night

It turned out to be a long night in that tiny room. Mr. Lily stayed with me the whole time, except for running out to check on Shawn every once in awhile. Shawn had fallen asleep curled up in the chair as reruns of *The Beverly Hillbillies* were aired. He didn't want to come into the room with me. Evidently this experience had been as traumatic for him as it had been for me.

The doctor that came in, Dr. Balli, was nice and she talked to me in a soft, calming voice. She was tall and thin, with long black hair in a ponytail that flopped from side to side as she moved about the room. Dr. Balli explained every step to me before she did anything, and asked if I had any questions. She asked me several times where my mother was and each time I just shrugged my shoulders. There was a concern that I didn't have parent consent to be treated, but my finger needed to be taken care of right away.

In the end, I had six stitches on the thumb side of my left pointer finger. The shot to make my finger numb was the worst part. I couldn't help crying when the needle went into my already throbbing finger. I didn't feel much when Dr. Balli actually put in the stitches, except I could feel pulling when she tied each stitch. Now it looked like I had a row of tiny black spiders going up my finger.

Dr. Balli told me to rest, and asked Mr. Lily to step out of the room. I closed my eyes and drifted off to sleep.

When Dr. Balli woke me, I didn't know how long I had slept. I looked around for a clock that didn't exist. I suppose they didn't want anyone to realize how long everything took in this place.

The number of people next to my bed had now multiplied by two. I saw Dr. Balli and Mr. Lily, but there was also a man in a uniform that I assumed was a policeman and a gray haired lady carrying a clipboard. Mr. Lily came around to my right side and put his hand on my shoulder.

Dr. Balli began, "Jack, we need information from you, and it's important that you are truthful with your answers. We care about you and want what's best for you." I didn't feel fully awake, but I suddenly realized that something big was happening here. I needed my best friend for this.

"Mr. Lily, can you go get Shawn?" I whispered. Mr. Lily let me know that he was sleeping, but I didn't give in. "I need to have Shawn here." I stated louder. He nodded, left the room and returned with Shawn, groggy eyed with his hair sticking out all spiky on one side.

"What's going on? Are you okay, Jack?" I showed him my spider-finger and he said, "Cool, can you shoot webs out of those little spiders?" I forced my mouth to grin a little. It was pretty funny, but I knew this was no time for humor.

Dr. Balli began again, "Jack, this is Officer Andrews, and our Social Worker, Inez. We can't have you go home without a parent. You said you don't know where your mom is and until we find her it isn't safe for you to stay by yourself.

Without thinking I blurted out, "I stay by myself all the time, and I will be just fine." I looked up at Shawn and he stared at me with his eyes bugging out. I figured that was code for - you should NOT have said that. A lot more questions were asked and at first I tried to back pedal and make up excuses for my mom. Shawn nodded and said uh-huh to everything I said, trying to back me up. Finally, it was just too much work and I was too tired. I gave Shawn a look of surrender, and then told my whole story.

It was easier saying it out loud the second time. Like I had rehearsed my lines with Shawn a few days ago, and now I was giving the real performance. It still hurt to hear the words, but it all spilled out to these strangers. Shawn was looking at me, trying to keep in the tears. We both knew this wasn't going to turn out well. Mr. Lily looked like he was in shock, listening with his mouth wide open.

When it was all said and done, they agreed to let me go home with Mr. Lily, calling him a family friend. Because he wasn't a relative, Mr. Lily had to agree to bring me to the Social Services office on Monday morning. Then they would figure out what would happen with me. Shawn, Mr. Lily, and I walked out of the hospital and into that parking lot without making a sound. We got into the car and sat frozen in our thoughts for a few minutes before Mr. Lily turned the key. The clock on the dash said 11:48. Almost midnight, no wonder I was so tired. Everything hurt, my finger, my head, my heart.

Mr. Lily pulled up in front of Shawn's house and asked if he was going to be alright. Shawn nodded and then he reached over and hugged me tight. I hugged him back, neither of us wanting to be the first to let go. We didn't know what words to say, so our hug did the talking for us. Finally Shawn let go, left the car and ran to the house. I watched as he used the key on his necklace chain to open the door and go in. My heart hurt more than my finger now, and I slunk down in the seat and closed my eyes.

Mr. Lily took me back to my house so I could sleep in my own bed. For the first time I could ever remember, I was tucked into that bed. Mr. Lily was going to sleep on the couch downstairs and he told me to holler if I needed anything. Then he told me in a quiet voice how very proud he was of me and that everything was going to be okay. I saw a tear slide down his cheek and I wondered if he really believed everything was going to be okay. I was too tired to ask, and closed my eyes.

The Weekend

I woke up to feeling a heartbeat in my pointer finger. I glanced at the six spidery stitches and memories began to flood my head. As I recalled everything that happened last night, I found it all so hard to believe. How could a night with chess and pizza with my best friend turn into such a disastrous evening? I turned on my side, curled my legs up, and held onto my knees. I kept thinking that once I got out of bed today, nothing was ever going to be the same for me. Maybe that was it, I should never get out of this bed.

There I was, rolled in a ball of sadness, just thinking about how I was going to be letting Zachary down if they couldn't find a foster home for me in Pine Hills. He was doing so much better in school, and I had been the one to help him do that. What now? Was he going to go back to crying all day and running away to hide? What about Shawn and Gran? I am going to miss them so much. We all need each other. I feel lucky that even though my mom has been absent from my life, I've had some pretty wonderful people that have been family for me.

That made me start to think about Mr. Lily, and how he had taken care of me last night. He had been there when I needed him, and he had been so kind about everything. I started to wonder why he had been at my house. Details about last night were such a blur, but I was starting to put it all together now. Mr. Lily was on the porch and had rung the doorbell. I was trying to see who was there, and that's why I wasn't looking at the pizza when I was cutting it. Had he told me why he was at my house? I didn't think so, but we were kind of busy with all the blood and stuff!

As I lay there pondering all the possibilities, Mr. Lily peeked his head into the doorway of my bedroom. "Are you awake, Jack?"

"Yeah, I kinda am." I groggily answered.

Mr. Lily came in and sat down on the edge of my bed. His hair was tousled and he had dark circles under his eyes. His nice white shirt was all wrinkled and stained with my finger-blood, and for the first time ever he wasn't wearing a tie.

"Did you sleep okay?" he asked.

"Yeah, I was so tired. My finger really hurts now, though. It's like it's beating out a rhythm." I used my elbows to push myself up in bed, and now was sitting up and able to look straight into his eyes. "Mr. Lily, why did you come to my house yesterday?"

He gave me a serious face and said, "I wanted to see if your mom was home. You hadn't given me her phone number, and I was thinking the signature on the field trip permission slip looked a lot like YOUR hand writing. I had the feeling that something wasn't right, and I wanted to see what was going on. I thought you might need some help."

I didn't want to tell Mr. Lily that I wouldn't have cut my finger if he hadn't rung the doorbell when he did. He was just trying to help me.

"Jack, I didn't realize it has been this bad for you. I wish you would have told me. You have been doing so much better at getting to school on time and everything you do for Zachary, well, I give you a lot of credit."

"Mr. Lily," I jumped in, "I have been doing so much better at school BECAUSE of Zachary. He gives me a reason to get up in the morning. I'm glad I have helped him, but he has helped me too. I learned how it felt to have someone care about you and need you. Spending time with Zachary has helped me to feel that. Knowing he was doing better at school, made me feel like my time with him was worthwhile, you know?" Mr. Lily smiled and nodded. "You, Shawn, and Gran have all helped me too. It's like you're my family. You all are the reason that I have been doing better."

Mr. Lily's eyes got watery. "Oh, Jack, I am so proud of you. You have really made the best of a bad situation."

I felt like I was going to cry, but I had to ask, "Mr. Lily, what is going to happen with Zachary now if they can't find a foster home for me in Pine Hills? Will he think that I just left him?"

He put his hand on my head and ruffled my hair, "I don't know Jack. I just don't know."

Mr. Lily left my room and I got dressed. When I got downstairs, there was a plastic bag filled with ice cubes for me to put on my finger. It hurt when the cold touched the stitches at first, but it felt much better when my finger went numb. I wished I could make my brain go numb right now, so I wouldn't have to worry about what was going to happen to me.

Mr. Lily did his best to keep me busy and make the rest of the weekend as fun, or bearable as he could. It didn't matter where we went, there was always that elephant in every room we went into. We worked hard to avoid it. First, we went to Mr. Lily's house so he could shower and change clothes.

Next, he took me shopping for some new jeans and shirts, and he wouldn't let me even help pay for them.

Then, we picked up Shawn and drove to Sal's Diner. Mr. Lily said we could pick out anything we wanted to eat. I told him I wasn't hungry, but when we went inside the restaurant and smelled the delicious smells, my stomach growled and I said I thought I would be able to eat something. Shawn and I both ordered bacon cheeseburgers and french fries, and became members of the clean plate club!

After dinner, Mr. Lily took us to the theater. Even though we were pretty full, we got popcorn and slushees. It was "Kid's Day" at the theater, and we watched an old school movie called, *Air Bud*. It was about a golden retriever that played basketball! It reminded us of some of the funny things Max does, and we couldn't stop laughing at times. I actually forgot about the elephant for awhile.

Sunday was Shawn's day with his mom, and I wanted to respect their time together. Mr. Lily took me to Zachary's house, and we played in his bedroom with his dinosaur models. He had a whole basket of them now, and he told me I could take my models back if I wanted. I told Zachary that I wanted him to keep them for me. That seemed to make him happy. I wanted to tell him that I might be away for awhile, but I didn't have the heart or words to do that today. While we were playing, Mr. Lily spent time with Zachary's parents. I wondered if he told them about what was happening with me.

When it was time to go I bent down and gave Zachary a great big hug. I was going to miss this little guy. Before I left the house, Zachary's mom and dad each gave me a hug too. They said they appreciated what I had done for Zachary and wished me good luck.

Mr. Lily said he had to stop home to pick up some clothes for tomorrow and then we'd be going back to my house. I felt bad he had to sleep on my lumpy couch again, and I suggested we stay at his house tonight.

Again, Mr. Lily said he wanted me to be able to sleep in my own bed. Probably, because it would be my last night sleeping there. He also said if my mom came back, she would want to find me at home. After we finally got back to my house, Mr. Lily suggested I take a shower to be ready for tomorrow morning. He had already called the school secretary and told her he wasn't going to be in school tomorrow. An emergency, he had called it.

When I got out of the shower and got my pajamas on, I found the new clothes that Mr. Lily had bought for me yesterday spread out on my bed. Mr. Lily peeked his head in and said I should decide which pants and shirt I'd like to wear for tomorrow, so I'd be all ready to get dressed when I woke up. That seemed like a good idea. Then I wouldn't have to scramble around to find clothes in the morning, like I usually do. I chose the lightest colored blue jeans, and a dark gray hooded sweatshirt. I put the other clothes on the top of my dresser, and kept those at the foot of my bed.

Mr. Lily tucked me into bed again and spoke quietly, "Sleep well, young man. We will handle all this together tomorrow. I'm there for you, no matter what happens." I know that was supposed to make me feel comforted, and maybe it did a little, but I knew that tomorrow was going to be a difficult day. Part of me wanted to crawl out the window and run and hide like I used to when things were scary or uncomfortable. I knew now that sometimes you just have to do what you have to do.

The Day

Monday was a long day. We sat outside offices in the Social Services building, waiting. We sat and waited in one waiting room before being called into an office to talk to someone. Then we were moved to another waiting area where we would repeat the cycle.

Most of the time the adults talked just to Mr. Lily. He was good about asking me if I understood what they said, and if I had any questions. I like that he cared what I thought. Everyone seemed to be in such a tizzy trying to figure out what to do with me, but by mid afternoon it looked like the only foster home that would accept a boy my age was about 100 miles away. Mr. Lily kept asking if they were sure there wasn't a foster home in Pine Hills, as he felt it was in my best interest to keep me in town, and in my present school. The response was always the same - no.

I was tired and hungry (we had only had snacks out of a vending machine), and this whole thing was making me mad. I had already used my breathing exercises twice. I could tell that Mr. Lily was feeling like me at times too, but he stayed calm and kept trying. Finally, the decision was made and I was going to a home in Akron Heights, where there was an opening that I would fill.

Mr. Lily was asked if he could take me home so I could pack my clothes, and then bring me back. They would transport me to my foster home. We walked out of the office with our heads fixed on the ugly brown tiled floor beneath our feet. We got out into the lobby and Mr. Lily guided me to a bench and we sat down.

Mr. Lily shook his head and got out, "I'm sorr...." but stopped and put his head in his hands. We sat there together on this bench, knowing that even though we were there for each other, the outcome was one that kept us from being able to speak aloud. Mr. Lily put his arm around me and we sat there, for each other.

At that very moment, feeling the lowest a person can feel, a gust of cold air blew in from the front doors being opened, and a flash of pink caught my eye. Could it be? There was Gran, decked out in a bright pink flowery dress, a cape adorned with sparkles floating in the air behind her. As she flew in, yup, there were those orange tennis shoes springing her along down the hallway like a gazelle. Shawn stepped out from behind the cape with the biggest grin on his face. When they spotted us they came running over, Gran hardly able to contain herself.

She was waving a big wad of papers in her hand and shouted, "Move over fellas, I am here to fix things!" She continued down the hall and straight into the office that we had just left.

Shawn came over by us, jumping up and down until Mr. Lily was able to get him to stand still for a moment. He asked Shawn to explain what was happening. "You'll see, you'll see! We have to wait, but you'll see!" Shawn sang out.

We waited and waited, and we couldn't get Shawn to tell us anything. He never stopped grinning while he kept alternating between jumping up and down and hugging me. Finally, Mr. Lily stood up and motioned for Shawn to sit down beside me. He continued to move even as he sat, his legs swinging wildly back and forth.

Mr. Lily paced the hall between the office and our bench. The office door was closed and I wondered if he could hear anything through the door as he kept moving in closer with each lap.

After what seemed like forever, the door burst open and out came Gran. She flew out as fast as she had flown in. She came over to the bench, then turned to face the gentleman that followed her out. His face was red and sweaty. He walked up to us and delivered the message that Shawn had apparently been working so hard at keeping to himself.

"Jack, it appears we have a foster home right here in Pine Hills that has an opening. Mrs. Halpa has so eloquently reminded me that she is a licensed foster home, but has never taken in a foster child. Somehow we missed seeing her in our files." I sat there flabbergasted, not believing what I had just heard.

"Zippity, Jack, what do you think?" Saying Gran was, "tickled pink," described her perfectly right now.

I couldn't get any words to come out, but I nodded my head as the happy tears poured down my face and dripped off my chin. I looked around and everyone, including the red faced man who Gran had evidently given a hard time, was crying. I stood up and hugged her with all my might, that pink caped Wonder Woman!

We were told the paperwork was all signed, and we were free to move my things to Gran's house as my official foster placement. When and if my mom was found, they would re-evaluate the situation, he said.

Gran was reminded of a bunch of rules, like someone would be coming for home visits each week and stuff like that. She assured the gentleman she would do whatever was needed to provide me with an appropriate home placement and gave him a sweet smile. She had put on bright red lipstick for her performance today and when she smiled, her teeth looked extra white against the red of her lips.

The four of us agreed to meet at the restaurant down the street to celebrate. Once we arrived and they found us a table, Mr. Lily ordered huge root beer floats for all of us. Then the details of this miracle began to unfold.

Shawn had struggled in school today. He couldn't stop wondering what was going to happen to me. He finally went to the nurse and said he felt sick and needed to go home. The school nurse called Shawn's mom and told her Shawn looked pale, his eyes had dark circles under them (the result of not sleeping well last night worrying about me), and maybe he was coming down with the flu. On his way home, Shawn stopped at Gran's house to tell her what had happened.

It was at that time Gran had sprung up and ran around the house shouting, "Where did I put those papers? Where did I put those papers?" Shawn said she looked like a chicken with her head cut off! Anyway, it turns out when Gran couldn't take care of Shawn when his mom went to the treatment center, she decided to go through the process of becoming a licensed foster home. She wanted to be prepared in case his mom would need to go back for more help. She said it had been so hard to see Shawn sent to Bay City. Once Gran heard about what had happened to me, she started searching for all that paperwork. Shawn said once she found it, they headed straight to the Social Services office, and the rest was history!

Who would have guessed that I would be staying with my adopted grandmother in a house that I already knew felt like a home. The happiness bubbled up inside me like the fizziness in the root beer! I looked around the table and saw three people that had been there for me when I needed help. How could I be so lucky? Now, I wasn't going to have to leave them, or Zachary.

Thanksgiving Day

Lying in my own bed, I looked around a room that was becoming more familiar each day. So much had happened in the past week. It was hard to think about sometimes, but the more I reflected, the more I realized how truly grateful I was. My life has been different than most people's. When I was younger, I thought everyone lived just how my mom and I lived. She didn't talk to me very much, and she would come and go. I learned not to depend on her, and to take care of things myself.

As I got old enough to go to school, I realized how very different that environment was. There was a routine, and expectations that I wasn't used to. It made me uncomfortable in the world of school where I didn't seem to fit. All the other kids seemed to follow directions and handle what was asked of them. I got mad at the teachers for expecting me to follow their directions and complete tasks the way they wanted me to. Didn't they know I never had to do that before? I was used to making my own decisions. I got mad at the kids. Why were they happy? They didn't seem to mind that there were rules, and they followed along with what was expected. I got mad at myself. Why did I seem so different in this place? Why couldn't I just fit in with the others and learn to do what seemed so easy for everyone else. Why couldn't I control my feelings instead of getting angry and upset?

I was the student that caused disruption in the classroom. I was the student that all the other kids were afraid of because no one knew when I was going to have a tantrum. I was the student that they talked about in the teacher's lounge. The one they couldn't figure out. I was the one that the principal had to come and remove from the classroom when I couldn't get myself under control. I was the one that went home each day to a house so empty and lacking in what a child needed. As I got older I learned how to control my feelings, and how to adapt and even appreciate routine and schedules and structure. I just wished it hadn't taken me so long to figure it all out.

So, am I angry that my mom didn't take care of me like I thought she should? You bet I am. I don't know why things have been like they have. Do I love my mom? You bet I do. I wouldn't be here without her. I choose to believe that she loves me and has always wanted the best for me, but she just didn't know how to make that happen. I often wonder what her life was like when she was a kid. Maybe no one ever showed her what "normal" looked or felt like.

There is an investigation now looking into where she may be. My hope is that my mom will be found, and maybe some of my questions can be answered. Maybe there is a way to help her be happy, and capable of being the kind of mom that a kid needs.

In my bed, thinking all these big important thoughts, I can hear Gran downstairs making noise with pans in the kitchen. She is preparing our Thanksgiving dinner for today. She has invited Shawn and his mom, Mr. Lily, and

Zachary and his parents. I look forward to us all being together, as it will be my first ever Thanksgiving dinner, on a day when I am more thankful than I have ever been.

After we left the restaurant the day Gran swept into Social Services and saved me, Shawn and Mr. Lily helped Gran and I move my things to her house. Mr. Lily thought it was important that I have my own bed there, so he was in charge of taking my bed apart and putting it back together in my new bedroom at Gran's.

Shawn helped me pack up my clothes, but that didn't take long. I looked around for anything else I wanted to bring. Other than one dinosaur model I found hiding under my bed, I didn't find anything else I wanted to take with me. Gran told me I could bring Alice. She said she was going to make her a soft bed from an old quilt, and buy her salmon flavored cat food. Alice was going to live like a queen!

After we put everything in Gran's car, I went back inside to take one more walk through my house. I stood outside my mom's bedroom door for several minutes. I didn't remember ever going in there. I opened the door and glanced around. There was the normal stuff: a bed, a dresser, and a rocking chair, with clothes scattered here and there. There was a mirror over the dresser, and as I walked over to look closer, I saw pictures of me starting from when I was a baby, all the way to my school picture this year. She had them tucked into the edges between the wooden frame and the mirror glass. I looked at each one, thinking about how much I had grown. I smiled, feeling happy that my mom saved all those pictures and had them right out where she could see them.

I heard Shawn calling me. I walked to the bedroom door and before closing it, I turned around and whispered into the room, "I hope you come back."

I ran down the stairs and told Shawn to wait. I rushed into the kitchen, and pulled a chair over by the sink. I had to step up from the chair onto the counter, but I was able to reach and take the twisted chicken clock down off the wall.

"This needs to come with me." I said. Shawn laughed as I jumped down to the floor and we ran out to Gran's car.

"What in the world?" Gran screeched.

"I thought we could put this up in your kitchen." I said with a sly smile.

After I stopped reliving memories in my head, I got myself out of bed and dressed. I ran downstairs to help Gran with making food for our Thanksgiving feast. It was fun being her assistant in the kitchen. She had so many different kinds of bowls, utensils, and gadgets.

As we worked, she told me about the recipes and who they had come from. She shared stories of Thanksgivings when she was a kid. She had put a huge turkey in the oven early in the morning and it was starting to smell so good! I could hardly wait to eat dinner!

Gran had me put extra pieces called "leaves," in the table to make it big enough so we all could sit together. I set the table with the plates, glasses, napkins, and silverware. Gran had made place cards with everyone's name on them and I put them on the plates where I wanted everyone to sit.

When I didn't think I could wait anymore to taste these delicious foods, the door bell rang. Mr. Lily was first to arrive with a pumpkin pie, and I played doorman to let him inside. I asked him if he had made the pie himself. He didn't answer, but gave me a smile and a wink! Next came Zachary and his parents. They brought a veggie tray with all the vegetables arranged in the shape of a Triceratops! It was so cool! Zachary hugged me and smiled his biggest smile. Not long after that, Shawn and his mom were at the door with a cranberry salad. Wow, I was thinking I needed an extra stomach to be able to try all this great food!

The next thing I knew we were sitting at the table. As I looked around at all these special people, I couldn't believe we were all here together. Gran cleared her throat and made an announcement that before we ate, we were going to go around the table, so each of us could say what we were thankful for on this very special Thanksgiving Day.

She started. "I am thankful to have my table full of wonderful people to share this meal with."

Zachary's parents agreed they were thankful I had come into Zachary's life to help him feel more comfortable at his new school. Zachary added, "I am thankful for dinosaurs, and for you too, Jack!"

Next was Shawn's mom, who said she was thankful to be home and have Shawn with her. Shawn thanked Gran for becoming a foster home just in case he needed her, but now so his best friend could stay in Pine Hills.

"I am thankful for my fourth grade teacher, Mrs. Worthington." Mr. Lily announced. "If it weren't for her, I don't think I'd be where I am today, which is exactly where I want to be."

Now it was my turn. I had SO many things to be thankful for. "I am thankful for ALL of you. Each one of you has made such a difference in my life, and because of your kindness, I am here today. Thank you for being there for me."

CPSIA information can be obtained
at www.ICGtesting.com
Printed in the USA
LVHW09s1005140818
586938LV00001B/5/P